My Adventures
with
Peter Pan

This story
was especially written
for
P J Mcateer
with love
from
Aunt Gwen and Uncle Greg

Written by Margaret Gibson
Illustrated by Ester Kasepuu

P J Mcateer woke up suddenly. He had been having a wonderful dream about pirate ships and mermaids in a make-believe place called Neverland. He heard a soft tap, tapping on his window. Opening his sleepy eyes he saw a little boy sitting on his window ledge. He looked very strange indeed.

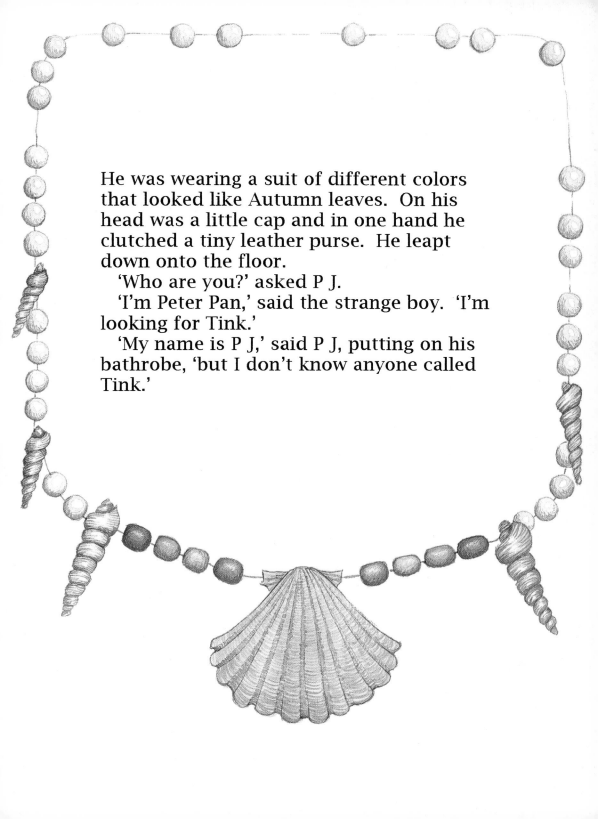

He was wearing a suit of different colors
that looked like Autumn leaves. On his
head was a little cap and in one hand he
clutched a tiny leather purse. He leapt
down onto the floor.

'Who are you?' asked P J.

'I'm Peter Pan,' said the strange boy. 'I'm
looking for Tink.'

'My name is P J,' said P J, putting on his
bathrobe, 'but I don't know anyone called
Tink.'

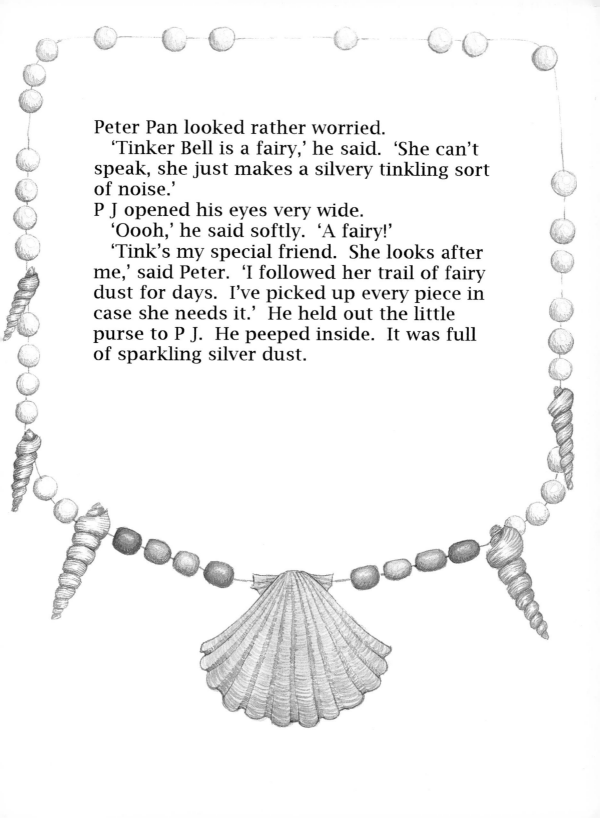

Peter Pan looked rather worried.

'Tinker Bell is a fairy,' he said. 'She can't speak, she just makes a silvery tinkling sort of noise.'

P J opened his eyes very wide.

'Oooh,' he said softly. 'A fairy!'

'Tink's my special friend. She looks after me,' said Peter. 'I followed her trail of fairy dust for days. I've picked up every piece in case she needs it.' He held out the little purse to P J. He peeped inside. It was full of sparkling silver dust.

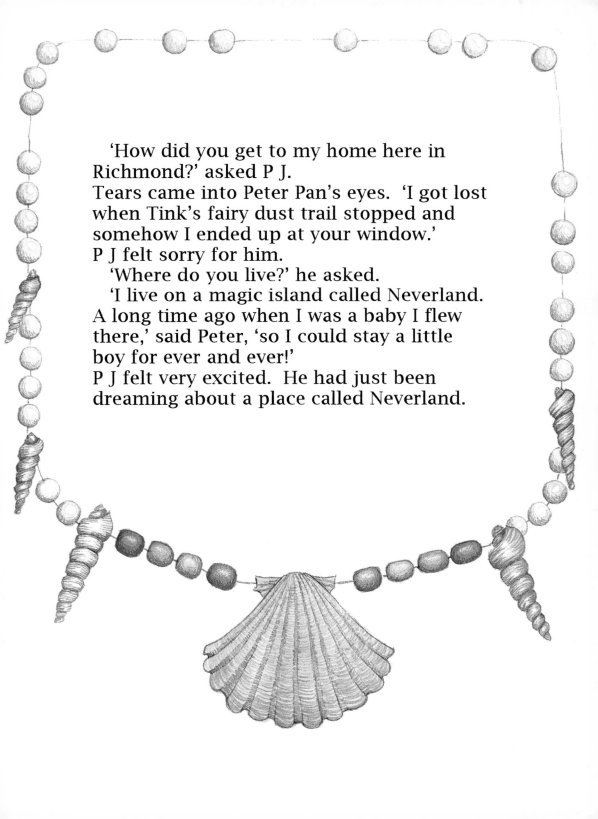

'How did you get to my home here in Richmond?' asked P J.

Tears came into Peter Pan's eyes. 'I got lost when Tink's fairy dust trail stopped and somehow I ended up at your window.'

P J felt sorry for him.

'Where do you live?' he asked.

'I live on a magic island called Neverland. A long time ago when I was a baby I flew there,' said Peter, 'so I could stay a little boy for ever and ever!'

P J felt very excited. He had just been dreaming about a place called Neverland.

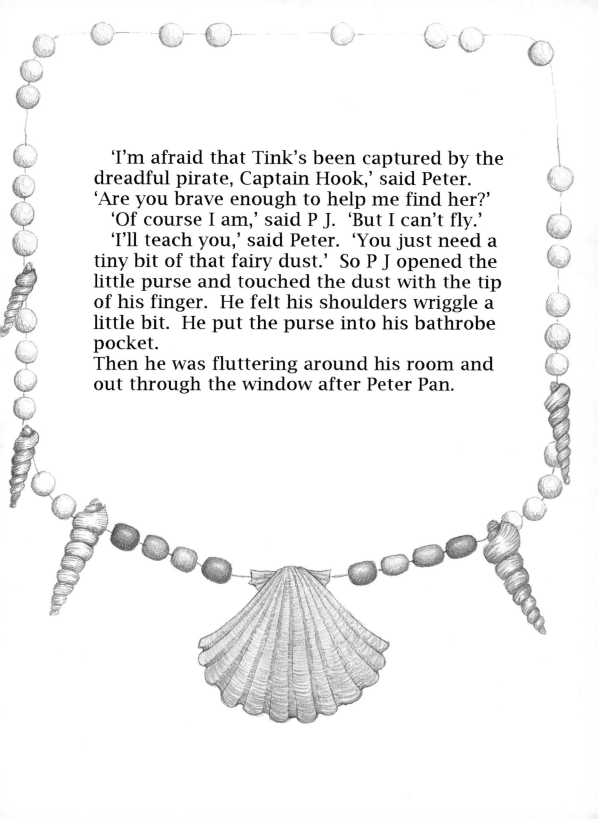

'I'm afraid that Tink's been captured by the dreadful pirate, Captain Hook,' said Peter. 'Are you brave enough to help me find her?'

'Of course I am,' said P J. 'But I can't fly.'

'I'll teach you,' said Peter. 'You just need a tiny bit of that fairy dust.' So P J opened the little purse and touched the dust with the tip of his finger. He felt his shoulders wriggle a little bit. He put the purse into his bathrobe pocket.

Then he was fluttering around his room and out through the window after Peter Pan.

It was great fun to be flying over high buildings and chimneys and church steeples and looking down at all the lights. They bumped against the clouds and soared high in the night sky. Soon they were flying over the sea.

'Now,' cried Peter, 'we must turn right at the moon and straight on till morning!'

'There it is!' pointed Peter. 'There's Neverland!'
Far below P J could just see an island. They
swooped down over the lagoon where mermaids
lay asleep on the rocks. They flew carefully away
from a large pirate ship, the *Jolly Roger*,
anchored on the far side of the lagoon. P J
followed Peter over the trees and they landed in
a clearing just as the sun was coming up.
  'Where do we start looking?' asked P J.

'Captain Hook has captured all the fairies in the world because only they can stop his evil deeds,' said Peter. 'He has hidden them away in a secret cave. Tink was the last fairy flying around.'

Peter told how wicked pirates had also taken the Lost Boys, who lived on the island with Peter, to work on the *Jolly Roger.*

'Tink and I saw the Lost Boys on Hook's ship,' said Peter. 'Tink was going to sprinkle them with her fairy dust so they could fly away. That's when I lost her.'

'We must find Tink and the secret cave,' said P J.

'Follow me,' said Peter, flying up into the early morning sky. P J wriggled a little and flew after Peter towards the blue lagoon. They could hear the surf breaking on the shore and see twelve mermaids lazing on the rocks, combing their long hair. P J and Peter Pan landed close by.

'Hello,' said P J. 'We're looking for Tinker Bell, the last of the fairies. Can you please help us?' The mermaids looked up and smiled.

'Many nights ago, we saw a little fairy flying near that horrible pirate ship,' said one of the mermaids.

Peter Pan frowned. 'Captain Hook *has* captured her,' he said. 'She must be in the secret cave with the other fairies. But where could it be?'

'We know all the caves,' said the mermaids, 'there's only one cave we don't go near.'

Peter looked very excited. 'Where is it? Why don't you go near it?' he asked.

'There's a terrible crocodile that swims near the entrance,' said another mermaid. 'The cave is over there.' All the mermaids pointed to the enormous rock on the far side of the lagoon.

'That must be the place!' Peter laughed. 'Hook hates the crocodile because it snapped off his hand and he has to wear a hook. It liked the taste so much it's been trying to catch him for dinner ever since. The crocodile also swallowed a ticking clock, so now Captain Hook can always tell if it's nearby.'

'You'll need some magic to protect and help you,' said one of the mermaids taking off her beautiful shell necklace.

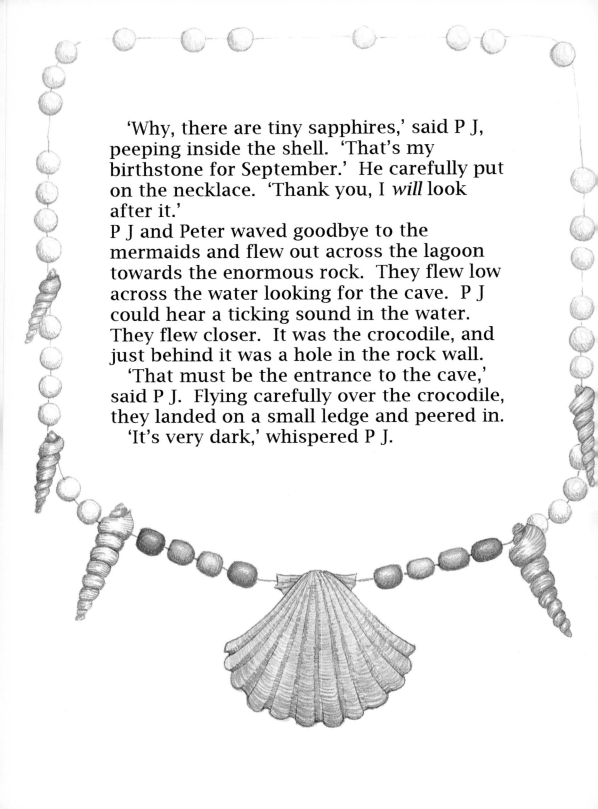

'Why, there are tiny sapphires,' said P J, peeping inside the shell. 'That's my birthstone for September.' He carefully put on the necklace. 'Thank you, I *will* look after it.'

P J and Peter waved goodbye to the mermaids and flew out across the lagoon towards the enormous rock. They flew low across the water looking for the cave. P J could hear a ticking sound in the water. They flew closer. It was the crocodile, and just behind it was a hole in the rock wall.

'That must be the entrance to the cave,' said P J. Flying carefully over the crocodile, they landed on a small ledge and peered in.

'It's very dark,' whispered P J.

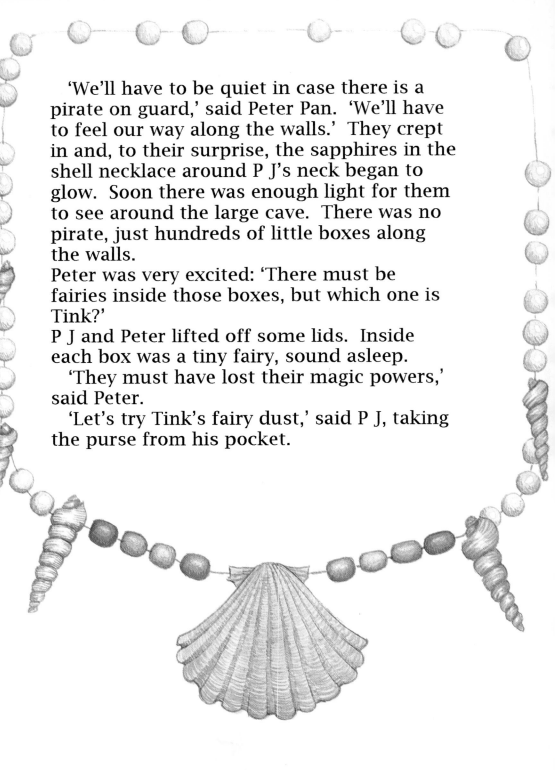

'We'll have to be quiet in case there is a
pirate on guard,' said Peter Pan. 'We'll have
to feel our way along the walls.' They crept
in and, to their surprise, the sapphires in the
shell necklace around P J's neck began to
glow. Soon there was enough light for them
to see around the large cave. There was no
pirate, just hundreds of little boxes along
the walls.

Peter was very excited: 'There must be
fairies inside those boxes, but which one is
Tink?'

P J and Peter lifted off some lids. Inside
each box was a tiny fairy, sound asleep.

'They must have lost their magic powers,'
said Peter.

'Let's try Tink's fairy dust,' said P J, taking
the purse from his pocket.

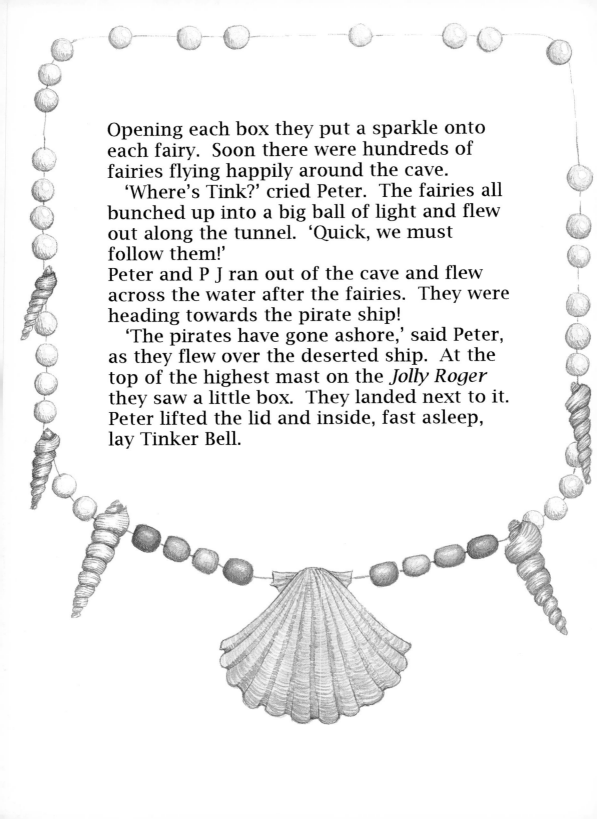

Opening each box they put a sparkle onto each fairy. Soon there were hundreds of fairies flying happily around the cave.

'Where's Tink?' cried Peter. The fairies all bunched up into a big ball of light and flew out along the tunnel. 'Quick, we must follow them!'
Peter and P J ran out of the cave and flew across the water after the fairies. They were heading towards the pirate ship!

'The pirates have gone ashore,' said Peter, as they flew over the deserted ship. At the top of the highest mast on the *Jolly Roger* they saw a little box. They landed next to it. Peter lifted the lid and inside, fast asleep, lay Tinker Bell.

'The fairy dust!' said Peter. P J opened the purse.

'It's empty,' he said. 'I'll try the sapphires.' So, very carefully, P J took off the mermaid's necklace and held it close to Tinker Bell. Once more the sapphires in the shell began to glow. Tinker Bell woke up and smiled. Sparkling fairy dust appeared around her and she flew out of the box. Tink was so happy to see Peter. She tinkled and flew around in circles. Suddenly she stopped and pointed across the lagoon. There were three longboats, full of pirates, rowing back to the ship.

'It's Hook!' cried Peter. 'Quick, Tink, lead P J and the fairies to the Lost Boys and set them free. I'll find some swords.'

P J and the fairies followed Tink down to a big door on the deck. P J turned the key and out climbed the Lost Boys. They ran to Peter who handed them each a sword just as Captain Hook climbed onto the *Jolly Roger,* followed by his wicked pirates.

'Take them, dead or alive!' roared Hook. A great fight began. Swords clashed. Soon Peter Pan and the Lost Boys had disarmed every pirate except Captain Hook.

'We meet for the last time, Peter Pan!' snarled Hook, and lunged at Peter with his sword. But Peter could move much faster and, before anyone could blink, the pirate captain's sword lay on the deck.

'Now you will walk the plank, Captain Hook,' said Peter, 'and Neverland will be a happy place once more.'

Hook backed away from Peter, along the plank that hung over the water. Just then, everyone on the ship heard the tick, ticking of a clock. Swimming beneath Hook was the terrible crocodile!

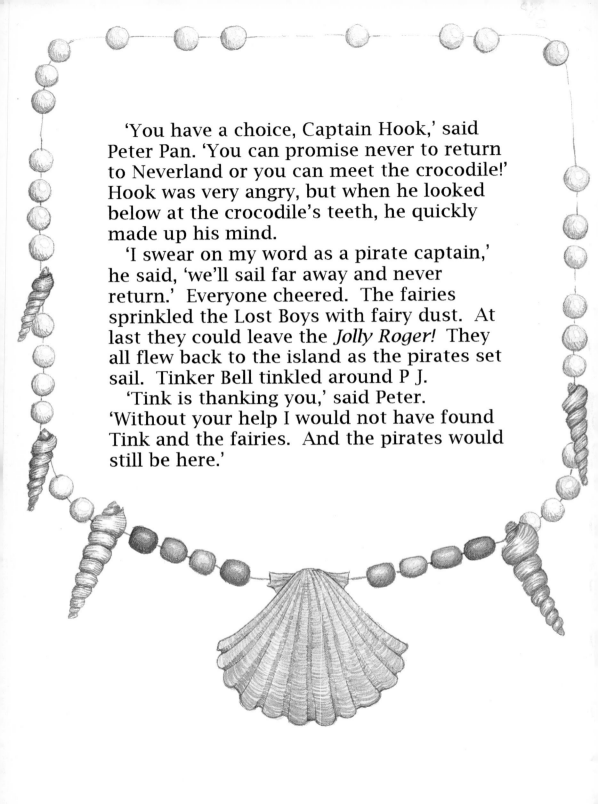

'You have a choice, Captain Hook,' said Peter Pan. 'You can promise never to return to Neverland or you can meet the crocodile!' Hook was very angry, but when he looked below at the crocodile's teeth, he quickly made up his mind.

'I swear on my word as a pirate captain,' he said, 'we'll sail far away and never return.' Everyone cheered. The fairies sprinkled the Lost Boys with fairy dust. At last they could leave the *Jolly Roger!* They all flew back to the island as the pirates set sail. Tinker Bell tinkled around P J.

'Tink is thanking you,' said Peter. 'Without your help I would not have found Tink and the fairies. And the pirates would still be here.'

P J felt very happy. Carefully putting the
necklace around Tink's neck he said, 'Could
you please return this and thank the mermaid
for *her* special help?' P J turned to Peter. 'I
think it's time you showed me the way back to
510 Greencastle Road, Richmond.'

'Follow me, P J,' he called, and they flew high
into the sky. Soon they were in Richmond at P
J's window.

'Thank you, P J,' whispered Peter Pan. P J
waved goodbye and slipped back into his bed.
He was soon fast asleep, dreaming of a
wonderful place called Neverland.